The Furchester Hotel™

Dino Hunt

It was early in the morning at the Furchester Hotel, but everyone was already busy busy **busy!**

"Furrr-gus!" called Funella. "Please take this towel to Ms Rrribbit for her swim!"

But Furgus was filthy from fixing the lift.

"It's OK, Auntie Funella. Elmo will do it," said Elmo, taking the towel.

"Room Two-two-two!" Funella sang after him. "Don't forget!"

Elmo stood outside Room 222, and called, "Elmo has Ms Rrribbit's towel for Ms Rrribbit's swim!"

"My swim?" came a voice from inside.

The door swung open.

"Ms Rrribbit?" said Elmo.

But it wasn't Ms Rrribit. It was a dinosaur!

"This is Room Two-two-three," said the dinosaur. "You want Two-two-two."

"Phoebe! Auntie Funella!" Elmo shouted, running away. "Come see! There's a dinosaur in the hotel!"

"A swim's not a bad idea," the dinosaur said to himself.
He grabbed a towel and headed to the pool.

When Elmo got back to Room 223 with Funella and Phoebe, there was no dinosaur to be seen.

They knocked on the door, but nobody answered.

"I hope he didn't check out!" said Phoebe.

"I doubt that, dear," said Funella airily. "Why would anyone want to check out of the Furchester?"

Back in the lobby, Elmo, Funella, Phoebe and Furgus gathered round the computer.

"Elmo thought Elmo saw a dinosaur!" said the baffled little monster.

"A dinosaur?" exclaimed Furgus. "I don't remember checking in a dinosaur. Do you, dear?"

"No!" said Funella, looking puzzled. "Look in the Who's Here file, Phoebe," she said.

Behind them, the dinosaur headed to the dining room. His swim had made him hungry!

"Who do we have staying at the hotel?" Funella asked, peering at the screen. "Betty Beetle . . . Harry Hound . . ."

"Got it!" cried Phoebe. "Mr Dean Dinofeller! It says here that he likes eating plants and walking in the rain . . . and he's staying in Room Two-two-three!"

Everybody looked at each other and screamed: "The dinosaur!"

"When did he check in?" asked Furgus.
   But before Phoebe had a chance to look . . .
   BONNNGGG! The Monster Teatime Gong sounded.
   "Teatime!" called the Teatime Monsters.

The Teatime Monsters stampeded through the lobby
to the dining room, almost crushing Mr Dinofeller,
who was on his way back to his room.

Ding! Ding! Ding!

Isabel tried to tell everyone she'd spotted
the dinosaur, but it was no good.

"It says here that Mr Dinofeller checked in a hundred and fifty million years ago," said Furgus. "That's a very, very, very long time ago."

"Oh no! That means I never got to welcome him to the Furchester!" wailed Funella. "This is a huge problem – we must find him! Let's put our furry heads together and think."

"Mind if me join you?" asked Cookie Monster, appearing from the lift. "Me great furry thinker!"

The monsters formed a monster huddle and made monster thinking noises.

"Me got idea!" cried Cookie Monster, holding some cookies. "Dinosaur no can resist cookie!"

"I'm not sure dinosaurs eat cookies," said Phoebe.

"Oh," said Cookie Monster, looking shocked. Then he cheered up again. "Luckily . . . me eat cookies! Om nom nom nom!"

"I've got an idea too!" Phoebe said. "Why don't we split up and look for the dinosaur in different places?"

"Brilliant!" said Funella. "Furchesters, start the search!"

The Furchesters searched high and low – they even looked under the ping-pong table! But nobody could find Mr Dinofeller.

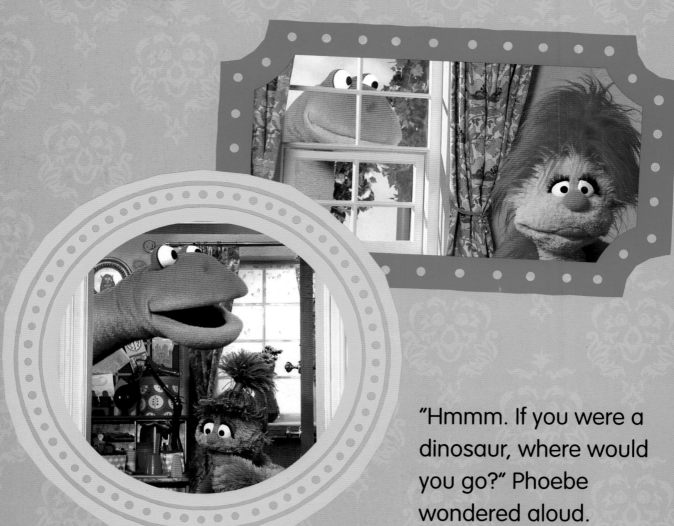

"Hmmm. If you were a dinosaur, where would you go?" Phoebe wondered aloud.

"Elmo the dinosaur would find Elmo's favourite food," answered Elmo.

"Fuzzawubba! That gives me a monster idea!" cried Phoebe. "The garden!"

The Furchesters headed for the garden, and crouched in the bushes.

"This is such a good idea, Phoebe! Mr Dinofeller loves eating leaves, and the garden is the perfect place to find some," Funella boomed.

"Shhh!" whispered the others.

"Erm – what are you doing?" asked Mr Dinofeller, as he strolled behind them, chewing a leaf.

"Looking for someone," replied Funella, without turning round. "Shhh!"

"A dinosaur," added Elmo dramatically, not glancing up either.

"Can I look too?" asked the dinosaur.

At last, Elmo turned round.

"Mr Dinofeller!" he gasped. "Everybody! Look! Elmo's dinosaur!"

"Well, Mr Dinofeller!" trilled Funella, hugging the dinosaur. "I know I'm one hundred and fifty million years late, but . . . we welcome you with furry arms!"

"Thank you!" Mr Dinofeller replied bashfully.

"Problem solved!" said Furgus, leading the guest indoors. "Come on, Mr Dinofeller. We'll get you a complimentary bottle of Furchester water . . ."

Elmo started to follow them, but then he spotted something big and dinosaur-shaped peering at him over the garden wall.

"Did Elmo just see . . . another dinosaur?" he gasped. He began to run. "Phoebe! Auntie Funella! Uncle Furgus!"